If your child struggles with a word, you can encourage "sounding it out," but keep in mind that not all words can be sounded out. Your child might pick up clues about a word from the picture, other words in the sentence, or any rhyming patterns. If your child struggles with a word for more than five seconds, it is usually best to simply say the word.

Most of all, remember to praise your child's efforts and keep the reading fun. After you have finished the book, ask a few questions and discuss what you have read together. Rereading this book multiple times may also be helpful for your child.

Try to keep the tips above in mind as you read together, but don't worry about doing everything right. Simply sharing the enjoyment of reading together will increase your child's reading skills and help to start your child off on a lifetime of reading enjoyment!

We Both Read: Jack and the Toddler

We Both Read® is a trademark of Treasure Bay, Inc.

Published by Treasure Bay, Inc.
P.O. Box 119
Novato, CA 94948 USA

Printed in Singapore

Library of Congress Catalog Card Number: 2010932585

Hardcover ISBN: 978-1-60115-249-7
Paperback ISBN: 978-1-60115-250-3

We Both Read® Books
Patent No. 5,957,693

Visit us online at:
www.WeBothRead.com

PR 11-10

Jack and the Toddler

By Sindy McKay

Illustrated by Jennifer Zivoin

TREASURE BAY

03175 2361

👓 "My friend Pam is coming over today," said Jack's mom with a smile. "And she's bringing her son Mark along to **play**."

"Hooray!" Jack shouted.

2

 "We can **play** ball!"

Jack's mom shook her head. "I'm sorry, Jack," she said, "but Mark is **too** small. He can't play with a soccer ball."

"It is **too** big."

   "**What**? You mean Mark is a baby?" Jack asked in surprise.

   Jack's mom chuckled. "Well, he's a toddler. But you can still **do** things with him." Jack held up Mark's picture and asked, . . .

 **"What** can he **do**?"

"He can do lots of things," Jack's mom assured him.

Jack wasn't so sure. Then he spotted his **pirate** hat.
"Yo, ho, ho!" he shouted.

"We can play **pirates!**"

Jack pointed to the picnic table. "We can use the table for a ship and sail the **high** seas!"

Jack's mom frowned in concern. "A toddler can't play on top of a table," she said.

"It is too **high**."

Jack's mom brightened as she suggested, "Mark's mom will probably bring a playpen. Why don't you use that for your ship?"

"No, thank you."

Jack remembered the new **paint** set he had received for his birthday last week. "I know what we can do," he said.

"We can **paint!**"

Jack's mom praised Jack for offering to share his new paint set, but she added that it might not be the best thing to do with a toddler.

"It is too messy."

"Why don't we put Mark in a high chair and the two of you can draw with crayons instead?"

"No, thank you."

"I know! We can all go to the park," said Jack's mom.

Jack smiled as he thought about the swings and **slides** and other play equipment. "That's a great idea," he said.

"We can **slide**!"

Jack's mom nodded. "Yes, you can! But Mark can't go on the big, tall, curvy slide."

"It is too fast."

Jack pouted. He loved the big, tall, curvy slide.

"The two of you can play in the sand," said his mom. "How does that sound?"

"No, thank you."

Just then, Pam and Mark arrived. Jack's mom introduced everyone, then turned to Jack. "Would you like to take Mark to your room and show him your big plastic blocks?"

 "No, thank you."

Jack's mom gave him a look that made it clear he had given the wrong answer.

So Jack took Mark to his room and showed him his **blocks**. "Go ahead, Mark," Jack said.

"Play with my **blocks.**"

Jack was not interested in playing with Mark. He picked up his soccer ball and began bouncing it off his knee. Mark pointed and grinned.

 "Play ball!"

Really? Did Mark want to play ball?

Jack put the ball on the floor and rolled it over to Mark. Mark rolled it back. Jack rolled it to him again. Mark rolled it back again.

🔈 "We can play ball!"

The boys played ball until Jack spotted an old laundry basket his mom had given him. Mark followed as he dragged it to the backyard and climbed inside. Mark climbed in beside him.

"We can play pirates!"

When they got tired of playing pirates, Jack's mom covered the picnic table with paper. Mark's mom covered Mark with a bib. Jack brought out his paint set.

"We can paint!"

Later the boys and their moms walked to the park together. They had fun digging in the sand and playing on all the play equipment.

"We can slide!"

Jack learned that a toddler can do most things that he can do. The toddler just has to do those things a little differently. And he realized that there was one thing they can both do really well.

 "We can be friends!"

If you liked **Jack and the Toddler,** here is another
We Both Read® Book you are sure to enjoy!

Just Five More Minutes!

It's Mark's bedtime, but he begs his mom for "just
five more minutes!" When his five minutes are
up, he keeps coming up with more things to do
that will take him "just five more minutes." Each
new thing is more funny and outlandish than the
last, including teaching a dinosaur how to tie his
shoes and brushing George Washington's teeth on
Mount Rushmore!